Robin Hill School

All Year Round

Read all the Robin Hill School books:

Robin Hill School All Year Round

Written by Margaret McNamara
Illustrated by Mike Gordon

Ready-to-Read
Aladdin Paperbacks
New York   London   Toronto   Sydney

ALADDIN PAPERBACKS
An imprint of Simon & Schuster Children's Publishing Division
1230 Avenue of the Americas, New York, NY 10020
The First Day of School
Text copyright © 2005 by Simon & Schuster, Inc.
Illustrations copyright © 2005 by Mike Gordon
Election Day
Text copyright © 2004 by Simon & Schuster, Inc.
Illustrations copyright © 2004 by Mike Gordon
The Playground Problem
Text copyright © 2004 by Simon & Schuster, Inc.
Illustrations copyright © 2004 by Mike Gordon
One Hundred Days (Plus One)
Text copyright © 2003 by Simon & Schuster, Inc.
Illustrations copyright © 2003 by Mike Gordon
The Counting Race
Text copyright © 2003 by Simon & Schuster, Inc.
Illustrations copyright © by 2003 by Mike Gordon
*The First Day of School, Election Day, The Playground Problem,
One Hundred Days (Plus One),* and *The Counting Race* were previously
published individually by Aladdin Paperbacks.
Designed by Sammy Yuen Jr.
The text of this book was set in CentSchbook BT.
This August 2005 Aladdin Paperbacks edition created exclusively for
Barnes & Noble Publishing, Inc. under ISBN 0-7607-7539-7.
Printed and bound in the United States of America
05 06 07 08 LBM 10 9 8 7 6 5 4 3 2 1

CONTENTS

The First Day of School

Michael loved his puppy.
Her name was Cookie.

All summer long,

Michael played with Cookie.

They played catch.

They played ball.

They were always together.

On the night before
the first day of school,
Michael said to Cookie,

"Tomorrow we start
first grade."

In the morning,
Michael walked to
Robin Hill School.

His mom and Cookie
came with him.

When they got to school,
Michael said to Cookie,
"Time to go to school!"

"Oh, Michael," said his mom,
"dogs are not allowed
in school."

"What?" said Michael.

"Nobody told me!"

He hugged Cookie tightly.

Mrs. Connor was the
first-grade teacher.
She saw how sad
Michael was.

"May I pet your dog?"
she asked.
"I guess," said Michael.
"He looks nice,"
said Mrs. Connor.

"She is a she,"
said Michael.
"Her name is Cookie."

"I wish Cookie
could come
to school,"
he said.

"Me too," said Mrs. Connor.
"You do?" asked Michael.

"Oh, yes,"
said Mrs. Connor.
"If Cookie came to school,
she could live
on the playground.

She could sleep
in a cubby.

She would belong
to everyone
at Robin Hill School!"

Michael gave that
some thought.
"Mom," said Michael,
"you can take Cookie
home now."

Michael had a good
first day.

But he missed Cookie.

When the day was over,
Cookie was waiting for him.

She waited for him
every day,
because she was his dog.

Election Day

There was a knock
on Mrs. Connor's
classroom door.

"That is our new student,"
said Mrs. Connor.

"This is Becky,"
said Mrs. Connor.

"Hello, Becky,"
  the class said loudly.
"Hello,"
  Becky said quietly.

Nia showed Becky where to sit.

"Can anyone tell Becky
what day it is today?"
asked Mrs. Connor.

"Today is Tuesday,"
said Ayanna.

"Today is election day,"
she said.

"Yes," said Mrs. Connor.
"Today we will vote
for our class
president."

After lunch,
the children gave speeches.
"I promise to get us
a candy machine!"
said Nick.

"Hooray!" said the class.

"I promise no homework!"
said Emma.

"Hooray! Hooray!"
said the class.

"I promise summer vacation
will last for six months!"
said Nia.

"Hooray! Hooray! Hooray!"
said the class.

"Would anyone else like
to give a speech?"
asked Mrs. Connor.

Becky thought
she could be
a good class president.

But she was new.

She did not have any friends.

She did not have a speech.

"Anyone?"
asked Mrs. Connor.
She was looking
right at Becky.

Becky took a deep breath.
She got up from her chair.

"I cannot promise
candy machines,

or less homework,

or more vacation,"
she said.

"I can only promise
to do my best."
Becky sat down.

No one said a word.
Especially not "Hooray."

"Now," said Mrs. Connor.
"It is time to vote."

The children put their heads
on their desks
and their hands in the air.

Mrs. Connor counted
all the votes.
"Becky is the winner!"
she said.

The new class president
was happy.

"You made a good promise,"
  Hannah said.
"It is a promise I will keep,"
  said Becky.

The Playground Problem

Monday was a sunny day.

It was recess.
Mrs. Connor's first-grade
class was on
the playground.

The boys were playing soccer.

"Hey!" called Emma.

"May I play?"

"No," said Nick.

"No," said Jamie.

"No," said Reza.

"We do not want you
to play with us,"
said Nick.

"Why not?" asked Emma.
"Because you are a girl,"
said Reza. "And girls
do not play soccer."

Emma was mad.

Emma was
very mad.

Emma was
FURIOUS.

That night she told her dad
all about the boys.

He helped her
figure out a plan.

On Tuesday
the girls ran out
to the playground.

They had a soccer ball.
They played soccer.

"Hey!" said Reza.

"The girls can play soccer."

"They are pretty good,"
said Nick.

"They are very good,"
said Jamie. "Emma! Come
and join the boys' team."

"No," said Emma.
"I do not want to play
   on a team with just boys."

"Why not?" asked Nick.

"Figure it out," said Emma.

On Wednesday
it rained and rained.

The girls played
at the activity table.

The boys sat
and stared at the rain.

"What are they doing?"
asked Katie.
"They are figuring
it out," said Emma.

On Thursday
it was sunny again.
The girls were
scoring goals.

"Hey, Emma!" said Reza.
"We figured it out."

"Boys and girls
can play together,"
said Jamie.

"They can play
on the same team,"
said Reza.
"We got it," said Nick.

From then on,
the boys and girls played
together.

Sometimes they played
really well together.

Sometimes they had fights.

"I figure that
playing together makes us
the best team
we can be," said Reza.

And he was right.

One Hundred Days (Plus One)

Hannah was excited.

Only one week to go
until the party
to celebrate
one hundred days in school.

"That is a long time
to be in school,"
said Hannah.

Mrs. Connor told the class,
"Next Friday,
please bring in
100 little things
to share."

Hannah decided
to bring in buttons.

On Monday, Hannah
found 20 white buttons.

On Tuesday she found
57 mixed buttons.

On Wednesday
she found
4 cat buttons,
6 diamond buttons,

and 13 buttons
with no holes.

On Thursday, Hannah
counted her buttons
from 1 to 100.

Then she sneezed.

On Friday,
Hannah had a cold.
"No school for you today,"
said her mother.
"On Monday you will
feel better."

On Monday I will feel
worse, thought Hannah.

The party is today.
And I am not there.

On Monday, Hannah's cold
was gone.

She wore her favorite
sweater to school.
It had one big orange button.

Hannah remembered
the 100 buttons.

She had put them
in her backpack,
even though she had
missed the party.

When the school bell rang,
Mrs. Connor said,
"Today is a special day.
What is one hundred
plus one?"

Hannah knew the answer.
"One hundred and one!"
she said.

"Right!" said Mrs. Connor.

"Today we have been in school
for one hundred and one days."
Hannah's friends were smiling.

They showed
101 grains of rice,

101 hair ribbons,

and 101 postcards.

"I only brought in
100 buttons,"
said Hannah.

"I did not think
   to bring in one more,"
she said.

She remembered the button
on her sweater.
"Here is my plus one!"
she said.

"I thought one hundred days
was a long time
to go to school,"
said Hannah.

"And now I have gone
for one hundred plus one!"

The Counting Race

"We are having
a race today,"
said Mrs. Connor.

The first graders
loved races.

"A running race?"
asked Reza.

"An eating race?"
asked Katie.

"No," said Mrs. Connor,
"a counting race."
"What is a counting race?"
asked Hannah.

"I am going to see
if you can count to ten
in one second,"
said Mrs. Connor.

"That is so easy,"
said James.

"I'll go first,"
said Michael.
"One, two, three, four,
five, six—"

"Out of time,"
said Mrs. Connor.

"My turn," said Neil.
"One, two, three, four,
five, six, seven—"

"Sorry, Neil,"
said Mrs. Connor.

135

"Me next!" said Eigen.
"One, two, three, four,
five, six, seven, eight—"
"Close!" said Mrs. Connor.

Hannah put up her hand.
"Mrs. Connor, can all
the first graders
work on this
together?" she asked.

"Yes, Hannah,"
said Mrs. Connor.

All the first graders
got together.

They talked loudly.

They talked quietly.

They had an idea.

"Ask us to race again,
Mrs. Connor,"
said Megan.

"Okay," said Mrs. Connor.
"Can you count to ten
in one second?"

All together,
the first graders said,

"Two! Four!
Six! Eight!
Ten!"

"You did it,"
   said Mrs. Connor.
"Good for you!"

"We counted by twos,"
said Emma.
"It is a faster way
to count," said James.

"Here is one more question,"
said Mrs. Connor.

"Two, four, six, eight.
Who do I appreciate?"
The children knew
the answer.

"Us!" they said.

And they were right again.